Midnight Magic
Witch Trap

For Sorsha
— MH

For Eira and your little black cat Pippin.
The best of friends already!
— EE

STRIPES PUBLISHING LIMITED
An imprint of the Little Tiger Group
1 Coda Studios, 189 Munster Road, London SW6 6AW

Imported into the EEA by Penguin Random House Ireland,
Morrison Chambers, 32 Nassau Street, Dublin D02 YH68

www.littletiger.co.uk

First published in Great Britain in 2022
Text copyright © Michelle Harrison, 2022
Illustrations © Elissa Elwick, 2022

ISBN: 978-1-78895-150-0

Printed and bound in China.

MIX
Paper | Supporting
responsible forestry
FSC® C144853

The Forest Stewardship Council® (FSC®) is a global, not-for-profit organization dedicated to
the promotion of responsible forest management worldwide. FSC defines standards based
on agreed principles for responsible forest stewardship that are supported by environmental,
social, and economic stakeholders. To learn more, visit www.fsc.org

STP/3800/0466/0522

2 4 6 8 10 9 7 5 3 1

Michelle Harrison ★ Elissa Elwick

Midnight Magic

Witch Trap

LITTLE TIGER

LONDON

Black cats born at midnight
Are **magic**, it's true!
Just waiting to have
An adventure with you.

Midnight and Trixie
Are very best friends.
When they're together
The **fun** never ends.

For Midnight is special:
She is **enchanted!**
All Trixie's wishes
Are easily granted...

Chapter One

It was October half-term,
A crisp sunny day,
The best kind of time
To head outdoors and play.

In the back garden
A mischievous pair
Were building their very
Own top-secret **lair**.

Snugly wrapped up in
Her coat, scarf and hat,
Trixie called out to
Her little black cat.

Her breath made a mist
In the brisk autumn air:
"Midnight, we just need
Some branches up there!"

Midnight winked up at
The out of reach place.
Magically, branches grew,
Filling the space!

They'd built their den out of
A pile of old wood.
And now it was finished,
It looked rather good.

"Done," Trixie said.
"Come on, let's go in!"
They **squeezed** through a gap
That was prickly and thin.

Oh dear, Midnight thought.
It's not at all roomy!
And even though they had
A torch it was gloomy.

How could she make it
Less dingy and poky?
She wiggled her whiskers...
The air became **smoky**!

Slowly the den filled
With shimmering light.
Sparks **fizzled** round it,
Twinkling and bright.

The smokiness faded.
To Trixie's surprise,
Their den (well, *inside* it)
Had tripled in size!

"Super!" grinned Trixie.
She peered through the gap.
Doodle the dog was there
Having a nap.

Nan was nearby
Planting bulbs for the spring,
Her feet tangled up
In gardening string.

Dad was at work
Piling leaves in a heap.
Their magic broom Twiggy
Was helping him sweep.

"We're **spies**!" whispered Trixie.
"I'll write what they say."
As Dad kept repeating
"It's *such* a nice day."

"It's code," Trixie muttered.
"Their talk of the weather.
These agents can't fool us!
We're **cunning** and **clever**."

"**Bother**!" Nan spluttered.
"I've swallowed a fly!"
By now, Trix was fed up
With being a spy.

Next they were pirates!

"**YO HO!**" they chanted

Digging up 'treasure'

That Nan had just planted.

Then they were prisoners

Locked behind bars!

After that, astronauts

Off to the stars.

After a while Nan
Was starting to ache.
"It's lunch time," said Dad.
"We both need a break.

"Trixie and Midnight,
You stay here and play.
We'll bring you some
Sandwiches out on a tray."

As Midnight and Trixie
Crawled from their camp,
They found their bottoms
Were muddy and damp.

"I know," said Trixie,
"Let's play hide-and-seek."
So she counted first,
Trying hard not to peek.

Now, WHERE, Midnight thought,
Is a good place to hide?
Aha! There's that leaf pile!
I'll burrow inside.

"Ready or not,
Here I come!" Trixie said.
But Midnight was sniffed out
By Doodle instead!

He snuffled and barked
Then happily leaped
Straight into the leaves
That Twiggy had swept.

Whoopie! thought Midnight,
Enjoying the chase,
And Trix jumped in too,
A grin on her face.

They rolled on their backs
And gazed at the sky,
Making leaf angels
As clouds drifted by.

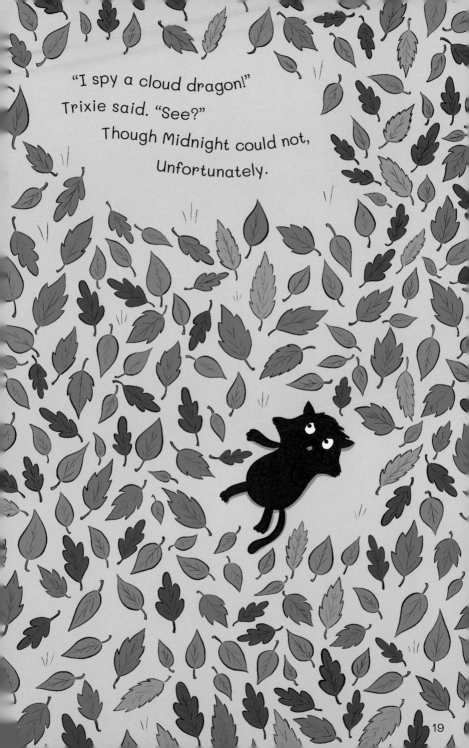

"I spy a cloud dragon!"
Trixie said. "See?"
Though Midnight could not,
Unfortunately.

But these imaginings
Made Midnight think
Of things she could do with
A magical **wink**...

A gust of wind blew
The leaves high overhead,
Creating a **DRAGON**
Of orange and red.

Whoosh! What a sight —
A *leaf dragon*, flying!
They both failed to notice
That *someone* was spying...

21

Chapter
Two

The leaf dragon landed
And flicked out its tail.
The tip was all pointy,
Each leaf like a scale.

It nuzzled at Trixie,
Its golden eyes wide.
They seemed to be saying,
Jump on for a ride!

So up Trixie scrambled,
Holding on tight.
With Midnight behind her,
The dragon took flight.

"Amazing!" cried Trixie.
She cheered as it soared
Then opened its jaws wide
And silently **roared**.

A jet of red leaves
Erupted like fire!
The garden grew small
As they flew higher.

Far down below them
Doodle was yapping.
The leaf dragon **swooped**,
Its scaly wings flapping.

Busy enjoying
The wind in her fur
Midnight caught sight of
A shadowy **blur**...

WHUMP! They collided
With *something* mid-air.
Midnight stayed steady
But Trix wasn't there!

She'd fallen right off
And was now clinging tight
To one leafy dragon claw.
Oh, what a fright!

"**Help!**" called out Trixie...
And Twig saved the day!
Catching their friend
In an instant. Hooray!

They all landed safely,
And Trix gave a shout.
"Look at that bush —
There are **FEET** sticking out!"

Of *course*! Midnight realized.
Crumbs, it was true!
Their dragon *had* bumped
Into someone — but who?

They wore pointed boots
And a fancy black cloak.
Then from the bushes
The somebody spoke.

"My, what a marvellous
Magical kitty!"
A **WITCH** clambered out,
Quite windswept and pretty.

She wore stripey stockings
And pinned to her cape
Was a silvery brooch
In a crescent moon shape.

"I'm Wendy," the witch said.
"And I'm fascinated
To see this fine dragon
Your cat has created!"

Trixie remembered
What grown-ups had said:
Don't talk to strangers,
Popped into her head.

Also, Dad warned them
They mustn't be seen
When Midnight did magic.
How **silly** they'd been!

But surely a *witch*
Wasn't likely to tell?
Not when she'd been flying
In daylight as well!

And just for a moment
It *almost* seemed funny...
Until she reached into
Her purse for some money.

"How much for the cat?"
Trixie gasped. "Pardon?
My cat's not for sale,
So please leave this garden."

"**Right-o**," chirped Wendy.
"I'm off, then. Goodbye!"
But there was a
Worrying glint in her eye.

She snatched her broomstick
From out of the dirt,
Saying, "How lucky
That no one was hurt!"

And then rather **wonkily**,
Wendy took flight.
Odd, Midnight thought,
That she flies when it's light...

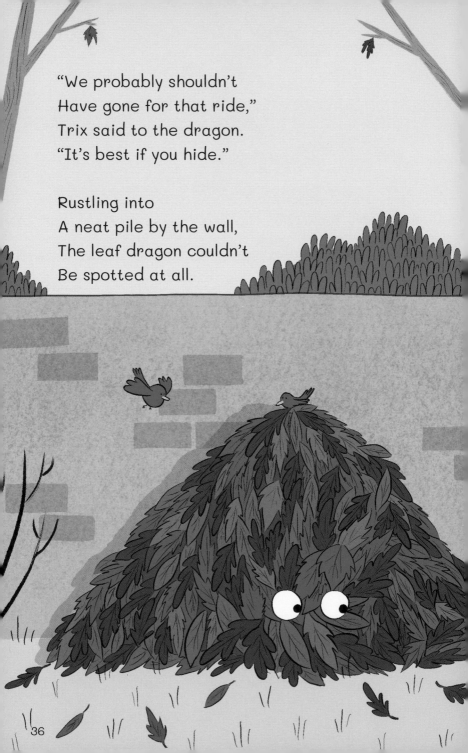

"We probably shouldn't
Have gone for that ride,"
Trix said to the dragon.
"It's best if you hide."

Rustling into
A neat pile by the wall,
The leaf dragon couldn't
Be spotted at all.

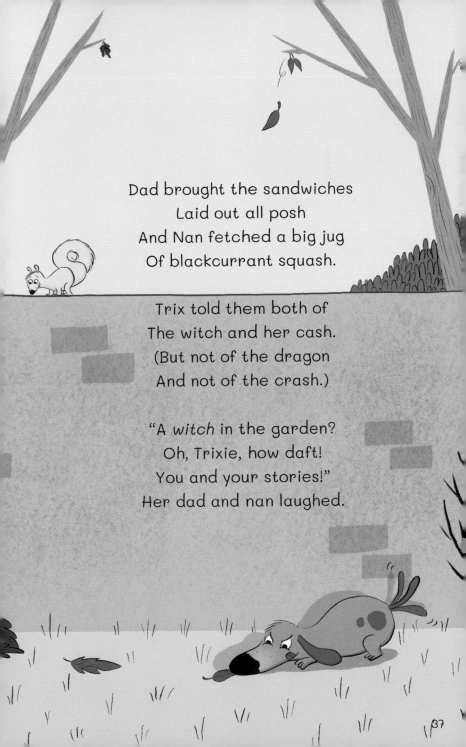

Dad brought the sandwiches
Laid out all posh
And Nan fetched a big jug
Of blackcurrant squash.

Trix told them both of
The witch and her cash.
(But not of the dragon
And not of the crash.)

"A *witch* in the garden?
Oh, Trixie, how daft!
You and your stories!"
Her dad and nan laughed.

"They don't believe us!"
Trix said as she chewed.
And after her lunch
She went off in a mood.

Midnight got up and
Went indoors as well,
Forgetting the leaf dragon
Under her spell...

But though it was nestled
Right under their eyes,
Nan and Dad didn't
See through its disguise!

Later that evening
When all were in bed,
And teeth had been brushed
And stories been read,

The dragon was curled in
A big golden heap,
Rustling each time that
It **snored** in its sleep.

Trixie was dreaming
And Midnight was purring,
But outside the window
A **shadow** was stirring...

Somebody wobbled
Up high on a broom.
With a magical key,
She slipped into the room.

She crept towards Midnight.
A floorboard went **creak**.
She trod on a hairbrush
And tried not squeak!

The witch held a cage
As well as the key.
"Kitty," she whispered,
"You're coming with me!"

Midnight's eyes opened.
Something had **SNAPPED**!
The lock on the cage —
Poor Midnight was trapped!

Chapter
Three

Trixie woke up and
She stretched out in bed.
"Good morning, Midnight!"
She sleepily said.

But no meow answered her,
No rumbling **purr**.
And when she reached out
There was no silky fur.

Trixie sat up, feeling
Suddenly chilly.
Why was she spooked?
Was she just being silly?

The *window* was open...
The room was all draughty!
Someone had been there —
Somebody **crafty**!

But there on the carpet
She spotted a clue —
A silvery moon brooch!
And then Trixie *knew*.

She raced down the stairs
Yelling, "Help! Something's wrong!
The witch has been here
And I'm sure Midnight's **GONE!**"

She showed Dad and Nan
The glittering brooch,
Describing the witch
Who'd snuck in to poach.

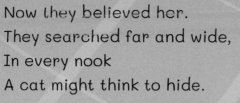

Now they believed her.
They searched far and wide,
In every nook
A cat might think to hide.

"Call the police, Dad!"
Trixie suggested.
"They'll track Midnight down
And have Wendy arrested!"

Dad rang right away
And tried to explain.
"A witch?" laughed the officer,
"Don't call again!"

"It's no good," said Dad.
He hung up the phone.
"**WE'LL** have to save Midnight,"
Nan cried. "On our own!"

"Let's split up," said Trixie.
She worked out a plan.
"Dad, you're with Doodle,
And I'll go with Nan.

"You take the car, Dad.
If Midnight's around,
Doodle might sniff her
From down on the ground."

"We'll go with Twiggy
And fly on ahead.
The view from above
Will help us," Nan said.

They took off on Twiggy
With Dad right behind.
Their mission was go —
CATNAPPER TO FIND!

But none of them saw it,
So none of them knew,
The dragon decided
To join the search too...

Meanwhile, a broomstick ride
Far, far away,
Midnight was having
A miserable day.

Trapped in the cage with
The magical key,
She'd tried to unlock it
But couldn't get free.

Wendy the witch shared
A ramshackle house
With Priscilla and Titch
(A toad and a mouse).

The shelves were full up
With big books of spells.
And bubbling cauldrons
Made curious smells.

The curtains were cobwebs!
And there, *oh good grief!*
Was a **spooky** piano
Made out of lost teeth.

"Sorry," said Wendy,
"About all of that.
But when I saw you
I thought, *I need that cat.*"

"Priscilla and Titch
Are 'familiars', you see —
Magical pets that
Help witches like me.

"I love them both dearly,"
She whispered, "However,
Priscilla's so clumsy
And Titch isn't clever!"

"I must have your help
To do my very best
And win the first prize
In the **Top Witch** contest."

Help her? thought Midnight.
*How cheeky! How sly!
No, I won't do it.
I won't even try!*

How she missed Trixie!
Her very best friend.
*If I'm to escape
Then I must pretend.*

She gazed up at Wendy
To say, *Understood!*
The witch tapped the key.
"You have to be good..."

The cage was now open —
And there was the door!
Could she find her way home
To Trix once more?

Hang on, she recalled.
Earlier this year,
Trix went to the beach
And got lost on the pier.

Afterwards Dad took
Some time to explain
What Trixie should do
If it happened again.

"If you get lost then
The best thing to do
Is stay where you are —
We'll come and find you!"

But how would they know
Where Wendy had ridden?
Could Midnight show Trixie
Where she was hidden?

There! In a cauldron
Of bubbling brew
Big **puffs** of smoke
Came from thick, yucky goo.

She secretly winked
And the witch's brew stirred.
Steam rose up the chimney,
Shaping a word...

Chapter Four

"The contest," said Wendy,
"Is one week from now.
I'll make a leaf dragon!
And *you'll* show me how."

She emptied a big sack
Of leaves at her feet.
But Midnight would not help
This naughty witch cheat.

*I'll teach her that I'm not
Her magical pet.
It will be a lesson
She'll never forget!*

She winked at the leaves.
The witch watched and smiled,
Expecting a dragon...
Instead they went wild!

They whooshed and they whizzed
In a terrible storm,
Buzzing round Wendy
Like bees in a swarm.

"Stop!" the witch shouted.
"You're making me dizzy!"
Good! Midnight chuckled.
That should keep her busy!

She winked at the spell books
Crammed on to the shelves.
They flapped and they fluttered,
Then flew by themselves.

Next the piano...
Although it looked eerie,
The tune Midnight conjured
Was charming and cheery!

Midnight peered into
A large crystal ball
And in it she spotted
The BEST thing of all.

Her family, searching!
Perhaps they were near?
She'd keep tricking Wendy
Until they were here.

High up on Twiggy,
Hopes fading away,
Trixie and Nan had
Been hunting all day.

Doodle and Dad tracked
Their broom from below.
Where could their cat be?
Would they ever know?

Up on the broomstick,
Trix said not a word.
And that's when the rustling
Of leaves could be heard.

"The dragon!" gasped Trixie.

"It followed us, Nan.

It wants to find Midnight

And help if it can."

They flew a bit further
Again Trixie spoke.
"That chimney down there —
It says 'HELP' in the smoke!"

"Clever old Midnight!"
Nan said with a grin.
They followed the smoke trail.
"We need to get in."

Trixie steered Twiggy
Up over the gate.
"Is Dad nearly here?
Perhaps we should wait."

"Let's go in right now,"
Nan said. "Dad can't be far.
We might lose our chance
If the witch hears the car."

"You're right!" said Trixie.
"I've got an idea."
She whispered it into
The leaf dragon's ear...

Inside the cottage
Wendy grew flustered
As down through the chimney
Leaves blew and blustered.

She'd *asked* for a dragon
But hadn't expected
More leaves to join up with
The ones she'd collected!

They formed a HUGE dragon
Right next to the door.
It lifted the latch
With a long curly claw.

Trixie rushed forwards
Past potions and charms
To quickly scoop Midnight
Up safe in her arms.

"*You* catnapped Midnight,"
Nan scolded. "But why?"
The witch went bright red
And started to cry.

"I'm sorry," she sniffled.
"It's rotten to steal.
But I needed a way
To do magic for real.

"My sisters are witches,
Much better than me.
They made this cage
And a magical key.

"I don't like the dark
So I fly when it's light.
I hate that piano,
I'm scared it'll bite!

"Your magical cat
Could have helped me come first
In the Top Witch contest —
I'm always the worst!"

Suddenly Midnight
And Trix understood.
What they could say to
Help Wendy be good.

"Your sisters," said Trixie,
"Are witches, but you
Should really choose something
That *you* love to do!"

Wendy stopped sobbing.
"You're right," she confessed.
"Reading my books is
The thing I love best!

"I promise I truly
Won't steal any more—"
Just then Dad and Doodle
Burst in through the door!

"Wait!" Trix explained things
To Dad in a hurry.
"Midnight is safe now,
We don't need to worry!"

All was forgiven.
They said their goodbyes,
Travelling home
Under crisp autumn skies.

Today, in the village
A wonderful store
Is full up with cookbooks
And stories galore.

Tucked in a corner
Is one little shelf
Where Wendy keeps spell books...
But not for herself!

Trixie and Midnight
Quite often pop by
To get books from Wendy
Or simply say "Hi!"

And every year
When leaves start to fall
A dragon returns
To visit them all.

A Note from Midnight:

Did you know that black cats like me are often the last to be picked from animal shelters? Sadly, it's true! People tend to choose cats with more unusual colours or markings. Sometimes black cats wait months — or even years — before finding a home.

So if you're thinking of getting a cat, keep in mind that black ones have just as much love to give. Some people even think we are lucky!

Remember to check out your local animal rescue centres, and give older cats a chance too. They can be just as playful as kittens!